Faebound

A Novella of the Otherworld

by
Jenna Elizabeth Johnson

Copyrighted Material

This is a work of fiction. Names, characters and incidents are a product of the author's imagination. All material in connection with Celtic myth has been borrowed and interpreted for use in the plot of the story only. Cover image is the sole property of the author. The *Faelorehn* font on the cover image and interior of this book was created by P.A. Vannucci (www.alphabetype.it) to be used in the Otherworld Trilogy. Any resemblance to actual persons is entirely coincidental.

Faebound

Contents

Faebound

-Part One-
Ghoulies in The Classroom

It's so very hard to be little, especially when you are little and unable to tell people what you are thinking. On the other hand, sometimes being stuck inside your own head can be a good thing. I can think better about stuff that way. Not the usual stuff everyone else my age thinks about, like when the newest episode of their favorite cartoon is going to air, or if their moms will let them go on a play date with their best friend, but the kind of stuff they don't notice normally. I think it's because most kids and adults are so distracted by all the noise and lights in the world that they miss the cool stuff.

Well, I guess 'cool' is the wrong word to describe it. 'Creepy' is probably a better word. Just yesterday, something creepy happened at my school. I don't go to the same kind of school my brothers go to, but I'm pretty sure weird little monsters don't just climb into their classrooms in the middle of lunch recess.

At normal schools, you have to talk to people and answer your teacher if she asks a question. Where I go to school, I don't have to do any of that. I like learning and discovering new things just fine, but at a regular school, I think the noises and the mean kids would be too much for me. Mom and Dad say that I have autism, and that's why I have trouble behaving like a normal kid. I don't know that much about autism, but from what I heard Mom and Dad saying when they thought I wasn't listening is that I have many of the symptoms.

At the time, I didn't know what a symptom was, so I had to look it up in Logan's dictionary. He's my older brother. It was hard pulling the dictionary from his bookshelf and even harder to find the word.

Faebound

I knew it was in the S section, but sometimes when I'm doing something, my body won't stop when I tell it to. Like looking for the word. My fingers kept flipping the pages long after I realized I had wandered into the T's. Other times, my body works faster than my mind, and I'll stop in the middle of doing something even when my brain is asking me to keep going. It is very frustrating, but I have learned to live with it.

When I finally made it back to the right spot in the S's, I read that a symptom is a sign that something is wrong. That had scared me. For a whole week, I moved around the house more carefully and quietly than normal. Being scared of something when you can't tell your family why is very hard.

Eventually, Mom sat down with me and gradually discovered the reason for my glum mood.

"Symptoms," was all I could say.

She must have realized I had overheard her and Dad, because she told me my autism made me different than other kids, but not sick or bad. She said the doctor was going to try to find some medicine to make me better, but that I didn't need to worry because she and Dad would look after me.

"Meggy?" I had asked, in a small voice.

Meggy was what I called my older sister, but her real name is Meghan. Of my entire family, I love Meghan the most, maybe even more than Mom and Dad. It sounds awful, to love your sister more than your parents, but for some reason I just do. It's like my heart has special little rooms inside for all my family and friends, but Meggy's spot is bigger than all the rest.

Mom had laughed at my question and kissed me on the head. "Oh yes, Meghan will always look after you, too."

And so, it was because of my autism that I went to a different school than the other kids on our street.

I didn't mind, and most days were calm with very little excitement. Except for what happened yesterday.

Ghoulies in The Classroom

Some days, we stayed inside during our lunch break and played with the toys in the classroom. Tuesday was one of those days. After we were done eating, Mrs. Warren excused us from our tables to go play. I went directly to my cubby and pulled out a comic book from home, the pages worn and creased from the dozens of times I'd looked through it.

I was just sitting down on the carpet when a foul scent wafted in my direction. I wrinkled my nose and instinctively looked toward the open window, my eyes widening at what I spotted there. Our classroom was on the second floor of the building, so the only things we ever saw outside were the trees at the edge of the lawn, the road beyond that and the birds that visited the feeders hanging in the oak tree nearby. But it wasn't a tree or a bird that I saw.

It was one of the ghoulies from my backyard. But what was it doing here? Ever since I was little, strange creatures that looked like half-rotten monsters had been showing up in my yard and the swamp behind it. At first, they had frightened me, but I remembered Meggy talking about them before I started going to school, so I figured everyone saw them. When my sister stopped talking about them, I thought they had gone away, but then they started showing up again. I waited for Meghan to say something, but she never did, and so I didn't either. I learned to watch her carefully after that, and I realized that she could still see them. She just wasn't telling anyone. I decided to do the same thing.

And now, one of them was hanging onto the ledge and peering through the open window. It had shiny skin, like a frog or some other animal that lived in wet places, and it was the color of splotchy mud. Long, crooked yellow teeth jutted out from its lower jaw, and its nose was upturned like a pig's. When I squinted, I could just make out a nasty halo of blackish red smoke radiated from its dark hide, like silt unfurling and forming clouds of color in clear water. All of these nasty things, the ghoulies, always had this weird color surrounding them, and they all smelled terrible.

Faebound

I would have been afraid, but like I said, I had seen them before. Not all of them looked exactly like this one, but I knew it was a ghoulie, and I knew it wouldn't hurt me. The other ones had stayed away from me the way mosquitoes avoid me when they realize I'm wearing bug repellent. Anyway, I was mostly afraid it might hurt my classmates. Just like everyone else, except for Meggy and me, they couldn't see it. As I watched it, the ghoulie shoved the upper half of its body through the window and was now reaching for the ground with its short front legs.

Click, click, click…

I jerked my attention away from the window and cast a glance at the girl, Maddie, sitting closest to me. She had pulled over a barrel of wooden blocks onto the carpet and was cracking them together, her glasses making her pale blue eyes as large as an owl's. The blocks came in many different shapes, the kind you used to make wooden cities with arches and columns.

One of the blocks, a rectangular-shaped one, had toppled away from the rest of the pile. I reached out, and ignoring Maddie's screech of disapproval, grasped the wooden block in my hand, my fingers clumsy and slow to respond to my thoughts. The corners were smoothed, and it was almost as heavy as a rock. I knew there was a risk of breaking the window if I threw it, but the monster now had its orange eyes fixed on Bella. She had an even harder time than I did communicating with normal people, and she couldn't move very fast. The creature would go for her first.

Sticking my tongue out in concentration, I drew my arm back and threw the wood as hard as I could, holding my breath and praying it didn't miss. To my great relief, the wood cracked against the creature's skull, causing it to squeal and jerk away from Bella, scrambling backwards through the window.

Mrs. Rodriguez turned away from one of the other boys, Jake, and glanced at the open window, then straightened and narrowed her eyes at the girl beside me.

"Maddie, did you throw a block at the window?"

Ghoulies in The Classroom

Maddie just grinned and continued to click the wooden blocks together, making a burbling sound as she did so.

Miss Rodriguez must not have been too worried about us throwing blocks because she looked back down at Jake. Or maybe it was because Jake had started flinging paint around with his paintbrush, and she needed to return his focus on keeping the paint on the paper.

Now that the scary monster was gone, I breathed a sigh of relief, one of the only sounds I could make without trying very hard. It was so frustrating. I knew how to read, and how to write, even if my letters didn't always turn out neat or facing in the proper direction. I could picture them in my mind, the words I wanted to say as well, but every time I tried to speak or print out a sentence, my throat would close up, or my mind would go suddenly blank. It was as if the string of words belonging to the sentence I wanted to write broke loose and went flying all over the place like deflating balloons.

My eyebrows drew together, and I glanced up, looking around the room and taking note of all of my classmates. There were only seven of us altogether. We were in what is called a Special Needs class. None of us were like normal kids, but that was okay. My mom and my teachers reminded me that I was extra special, and that's why I couldn't go to a school like my brothers or sister.

Knowing all this didn't bother me. I didn't want to be like the normal kids. Bradley and Logan had told me stories about some of the kids at their school who were mean to them and the other students. The nice thing about my school was that all my classmates usually got along, and none of them ever did anything just to be mean. Even so, something, some feeling deep inside of me, told me that I was very different from my fellow classmates as well. Seeing the ghoulies was only part of it.

Maddie made a loud noise, and I jumped, breaking out of my own personal reflection. When I looked up at her, she was smiling and holding out one of the wooden arches.

I tried smiling back. She was asking me if I would help her build a city. Deciding it was best for me to forget about the monster in the window, I took the block and scooted closer to her. As I started stacking wooden shapes with as much coordination as my hands would allow me, I thought about some of the other reasons I was different. I created a bridge with one of the larger arches and glanced up at my friend.

Maddie didn't glow like me. Neither did Jake, Russell, Bella or Mira. Mrs. Warren and her assistant, Miss Rodriguez, didn't glow, either. In fact, most people didn't glow. Just me and my sister, Meghan. When I was little, I didn't think too much about it. But now that I was seven, I wondered about stuff all the time. Not just why we glowed, but also why we saw the ghoulies, and no one else did.

I sighed and got back to building castles with Maddie. Thinking about monsters reminded me of the ghoulie from earlier. I still had no idea why it had showed up here, or why it was out during the day. Usually, I only saw them before and after sunset. Trying to forget about it, I picked up a cone-shaped block and was about to add it to the top of a turret when a shadow momentarily blocked the light streaming in through the window. I glanced up, my hand freezing in mid-air like a crane jerking to a stop over a half-constructed skyscraper. The ghoulie from earlier was back, its wicked claws scratching at the corner of the ledge, trying to find purchase on the windowsill.

My mouth went dry, and my skin grew hot. I risked a glance at my arm. Just as I suspected, the pale blue glow of my skin had grown a little brighter. This always scared me. It happened a lot when I was frightened or mad or sad. Each time it happened, I was worried my skin might actually melt, but I always managed to calm down before it grew worse.

I returned my attention to the window and nearly gasped. A second ghoulie had joined the other and was trying to force its way in as well. And then, a third one appeared, its beady eyes fierce and glowing orange as it peered at me through the window. The fear crept over my skin like icy spiders, and I tried to remain calm. Why were there so many? What were they doing out in the middle of the day? And then, I remembered: Halloween was only three days away. That would explain why there were so many, but not why they were here.

Halloween night had always made me nervous, ever since before I could walk. Mom or Meghan would help me make my costume, and then, I'd go out trick-or-treating with my brothers and sister, just like all the other kids. I would laugh and scream and try to look like I was having a good time. That's what grown-ups expected of kids on Halloween. Only, that was the one time of year that the ghoulies came out the most. Kind of like the way worms crawl out onto the sidewalks after a rainstorm. Even if they could never get close enough to hurt me, they still scared me and gave me bad dreams.

The slight rustle of cloth distracted me from the creatures scrabbling at the windowsill. Mari, who had been completely absorbed in her picture book over in the library nook, had flung the book down and was making a bee line for the window.

For a few seconds, I sat gaping at her. Could she see the monsters, too? I returned my eyes to the window. One of the ghoulies had pulled its attention away from the classroom and was busy eyeing a hummingbird buzzing around the feeder in the oak tree.

"Hummie, hummie!" Mari squealed, her hands outstretched as she moved closer to the window.

Without giving it a second thought, I dropped the block I was holding. It crashed down and crumbled the castle in progress into a pile of rubble. Maddie gasped, then made a sound of outrage, but I hardly noticed. I was too busy making my way to the window.

Look out! I wanted to shout. *The ghoulies will hurt you!* But all that came out was, "Goos! Hurt!"

With my heart racing in time with my feet, I shoved Mari out of the way and reached for the window latch. The girl went down screeching, crying at the top of her lungs when her bottom hit the ground.

The monsters latched their attention onto me, their predatory eyes narrowing as they bared their teeth and hissed. One of them had slipped its arm through the open window and was trying to sink its claws into the wall.

Panicking, I spun around, trying to find something to use as a weapon against it. A shelf of books, some bean bag chairs, the table with our math activity from earlier …. A cup of pencils sat on the bookshelf closest to me. As quickly as I could, I reached out and grabbed one of the largest pencils, nearly shouting in triumph as my thoughts and actions worked in unison for once. The tip was dull from use, and the eraser was worn all the way down to the metal band, but it would have to do.

Another sharp hiss, followed by a growl, caught my attention, and I spun back around. The first ghoulie had wedged the window open further and had stuck its head through, its pig nose sniffing the air. It glared at me, but couldn't swipe me with its claws because both front feet were being used to hang onto the windowsill. The smell coming off it made me gag, and I held my arm up to my nose. The monster lunged again, and the others behind it forgot all about the hummingbird as they turned to regard me and the other students once again.

A fresh shriek of anger and pain from Mari had drawn the attention of our teachers. Mrs. Warren and Miss Rodriguez were now looking in our direction with worry on their faces. I continued to stare at the three ghoulies, scraping my brain for any sort of idea that might make them go away. They were still struggling, but it wouldn't be long before they made it into the classroom, especially since the first one had almost succeeded earlier. I didn't have much time. Taking a deep breath and telling myself to be brave, I turned the pencil around, pointy end out, and shoved it as hard as I could into the eye of the closest ghoulie.

The beast screeched in pain and let go of the windowsill to claw at its eye. The others, who had mostly been hanging onto the first one, wheeled back and the whole lot of them crashed to the ground below. Taking a shaky breath, I stepped forward, almost falling over my own feet, and pulled the window shut. It clicked into place, and I fumbled with the latch until it locked.

By that time, both Mrs. Warren and Miss Rodriguez were kneeling beside Mari to see if she had hurt herself. The dark-haired girl mumbled something and pointed in my direction. Her face was scarlet, and there were streaks of tears painting her cheeks.

"Aiden?" Miss Rodriguez asked softly, "Did you push Mari down?"

I stood still, my hands clamped behind my back, and hung my head. It was times like these that I really wished I could talk like normal kids.

I nodded my head. Even if I couldn't communicate like everyone else, I never lied. Mom had told me that lying made you weaker, and being honest made you stronger, even if it was hard to be honest.

I was already weak in so many ways. I wanted to be strong, so I never lied.

"Why?" Mrs. Warren pressed.

I looked up toward the window. Blackish streaks and a few scratches showed on the wall, but like the creatures, I knew I was the only one who noticed the marks. I wanted to tell them about the ghoulies, but I knew telling people you saw scary monsters that no one else could see was worse than lying. Instead, I told them something else that may not have been entirely truthful, but wasn't really a lie either.

There was something dangerous trying to get in through the window, a wasp I think. Mari was distracted by the hummingbird and didn't see it, so I pushed her, so she wouldn't get stung. Then I closed the window, so it wouldn't get inside.

That's what I would have said if I could. Instead, I opened my mouth and tried to speak. After a long while, all that came out was, "Wasp near window. Help."

I wanted to cry. Not because I thought I was in trouble, or even because I felt bad for knocking Mari down, but because I couldn't tell my teachers what had happened. I couldn't even apologize properly to Mari for being so rude. But I did try.

Turning toward my classmate, I mumbled, "Sworry," and offered her my hand.

She stared at it with big brown eyes and sniffed once before reaching out her own hand to accept my help. Her fingers were wet, but I knew it was because of her tears.

"Thankoo, Aiden," she said, her rage and tears suddenly gone.

She smiled at me and gave me a hug, which made me blush. Mom was always teasing me by saying that Mari had a crush on me, and now I was beginning to wonder if saving her from the ghoulies had made it worse.

"Next time, you need to get one of us if you see any wasps," Mrs. Warren said, her voice more stern than before.

Both she and Miss Rodriguez got up and returned to their previous tasks. Taking a deep breath and letting it out, I shuffled back over to Maddie and helped her pick up the blocks. I expected her to be angry with me as well, but during the whole incident at the window, she managed to start building the castle's foundation once again.

For five more minutes, I helped with the blocks until Miss Rodriguez rang the bell announcing our lunch break was over. We all put back our toys and games and then headed to our cubbies where our pillows and blankets were stored. I recovered my comic book and put it back as well.

"Alright boys and girls!" Mrs. Warren proclaimed. "Nap time!"

Jake and Mari groaned, but Maddie and Bella started rolling out their blankets. Russell refused to follow directions at first, but then Miss Rodriguez went over to encourage him to join the rest of the class. Not wanting to draw any more attention to myself, I did as I was told, smoothing out the corners of my small quilt and fluffing my pillow. I especially loved my pillow because my sister had bought it for me.

"It's green and extra soft," she'd told me when she brought it home with Mom one day. "And I even got a little pouch full of dried lavender to put inside the pillowcase to help you sleep."

Logan and Bradley had laughed and told me it made me smell like a girl, but I didn't care. Meggy had got it for me.

As I lay still, listening to the relaxing music Miss Rodriguez had put on for us, I breathed in deeply, the faint scent of lavender tickling my nose. The smell reminded me of my big sister, and thinking of Meghan made me feel much better. Soon, the scary images of the ghoulies faded from my mind, and I fell asleep.

-Part Two-

Black Bird

Mom picked me up later that afternoon. She worked at one of the local high schools and had a different schedule than most teachers. Some days, she had to go to work early and got to come home early. Other days, she started late and picked me up later. My school, like me, wasn't normal. At least, not really. I didn't have to be in class at the same time every day. Mom could drop me off on her way to work and pick me up when she got off, whenever that happened to be. Today, she picked me up just before two o'clock.

Mom talked with Miss Rodriguez for a few minutes before turning toward me. "Ready to go home, Aiden?"

She smiled and held out a hand as I rubbed at my eyes, trying to wipe away the sleepiness. On most days, I didn't have any trouble sleeping during nap time. Today, I could only lie there and stare at the window, my stomach tying itself into knots as I waited for the ghoulies to come back.

I nodded my head as I got closer to Mom, reaching up to take her hand. Her fingers were warm and strong, and she held onto mine as if she d never let go.

Downstairs, her car waited in one of the slots in the parking lot. As we passed under the window to my classroom, I held my breath, expecting to see the ghoulies hiding in the bushes. Either they were gone for good, or they were staying out of sight because I didn't see them as I climbed into the backseat of Mom's car. Maybe I had imagined the whole thing, after all. Maybe I really *had* slept during nap time, and I had only dreamed the whole thing.

Black Bird

"How was school today?" Mom asked, her eyes watching me in the rear-view mirror.

Feeling somewhat ashamed about the ghoulies, I lowered my eyes and studied my hands. I couldn't tell her about it even if I wanted to. Even now, as I tried to put the thoughts together in my mind, they buckled against some invisible barrier, the way a soda can crunches and folds up when one of my older brothers steps on it.

When I didn't answer her, Mom took a deep breath and released it on a sigh. "I talked to Dr. Sellers on the phone this morning. She says she has some medicine she wants to try out with you. To see if it will make you feel better when you get upset."

Mom's voice trailed off at the end, and I felt my fingers curl into fists. When she said she wanted to make me feel better, she meant the times I had my fits. Even though I couldn't talk like my brothers and sister, I had no trouble letting them know I was angry, frustrated or scared about something. Usually, I only got mad or upset when the ghoulies came around because I was afraid they'd hurt Jack, Joey, Logan and Bradley, or even Meghan. And because I could do nothing, I would throw what Bradley called 'temper tantrums'. My doctor said it was common for children with autism to 'express aggression'. I didn't really know what those words meant, but I could tell Dr. Sellers had been talking about my fits.

My parents didn't talk too much about my autism with me, but they always let me know what they planned to do to help me with it. In this world, kids were expected to be able to do certain things at certain ages. Since I was seven, I should be able to read and write sentences and add and subtract numbers, as well as many other things, including getting along with other kids. I could read, and I could add and subtract just fine. But, I couldn't prove it to my parents or my teachers. My fingers wouldn't hold a pencil like they should, so I couldn't write my name down or show them that eight plus two was ten. When I snuck into my older brothers' room and took their chapter books from the bookshelves, it wasn't just because I liked the sound of the paper fluttering as I flipped the pages.

Faebound

Despite what my family thought, I liked the books because they were about awesome adventures with dragons and magicians and superheroes. But if I were to open my mouth to say the words out loud, nothing ever came out. Once in a while, one or maybe two words would break free, but then, my throat would clog up or my tongue would get stuck to the roof of my mouth. I couldn't explain it. It was like the real me was living inside a glass ball made of a mirror that only I could see out of, but no one else could see in. I wondered if that's what it was like for my other classmates too, but I had no way of asking them.

Before I ever started school, Mom used to take me to therapy with other moms who had kids like me. We would learn what the teacher called 'social skills'. I didn't learn much there because most of the stuff they taught us I already knew from listening to Mom and Dad talk to Bradley, Logan and Meghan. Sighing, I thought about what Mom had said about taking medicine. Part of me felt nervous about it, and another part of me felt guilty that, no matter how hard they tried, Mom and Dad and the doctors couldn't seem to help me get better.

Eventually, I looked up, only to find Mom glancing at me in the rearview mirror. She looked worried, and I wondered why. Mom always got this way after talking to the doctor. I turned my eyes quickly away once again and stared out the window. The trees lining the road were just starting to change color, and some of them had already lost most of their leaves, their bare white branches like the hands of skeletons.

Mom flicked on her turn signal, and our car rolled to a stop as she approached a traffic light. On the left, a large shopping center sat partially hidden behind a row of neatly trimmed hedges. I peeked up between the two front seats and glanced out the windshield. Traffic rushed by in a hurry, each car that flew by making ours rock a little. Mom was taking the back road home today, and I smiled. I liked the fast roads, but the freeway always scared me a little. It felt like we were driving on a racetrack with all those other cars, some of them really big, but on the highways, we could still go fast and there were only two lanes most of the time. No big scary trucks taking forever to pass you if you were stuck behind a slow driver.

The light turned green, and Mom pulled forward, turning right after the car in front of her crossed the intersection. We quickly picked up speed, and I glanced out the window once again, smiling when we passed the airport. A small plane was landing as we drove by, its wing lights blinking like little stars.

The open, rolling landscape of rural San Luis Obispo was blanketed with acres of vineyards, the golden leaves of the grapevines a cheerful, sunny yellow splashed against the blue sky. An occasional farm house, complete with a paddock for horses or goats, helped add variety to the scenery. Just as I was starting to put the bad memories of the day behind me, I noticed a pumpkin patch coming up on the left. The orange gourds, glowing like burnished beads in the afternoon sunlight, reminded me, once again, Halloween was only a few days away. Normally, the sight of pumpkins wouldn't bother me, but the small, rustic shed set up nearby had one of those giant blow up jack-o-lanterns next to it, the black slash of its eyes and mouth reminding me of the ghoulies.

I jerked my head to the side and glanced out the other window, quickly trying to banish the memories. We had come to another traffic stop, and as Mom waited for the light to change, a crow came to rest on a fence post on the side of the road. It turned its head, one black, glossy eye staring at me. A red sheen flashed over the bird's eye, and a sharp pain pierced my head. Drawing in a quick breath, I squeezed my eyes shut. A memory, harsh as corrosive acid spilling against the backs of my eyes, flooded my mind, and a kaleidoscope of scenes played out in my head. A huge black bird with burning red eyes ... Weird, dark red smoke curling in unnatural tendrils around a tree ... A terrifying voice speaking in my head ... Where had these memories come from? Tangled up with all the images was another memory, one of my sister cutting her hand in the kitchen. Yesterday. Meghan had hurt herself yesterday. Were these memories from the same time? I felt my face pale, and my heart begin to race. What was going on?

Faebound

The light changed, and our car quickly picked up speed, leaving the crow behind. Clenching my teeth, I squeezed my eyes shut and tried very hard to remember everything that had happened yesterday. I had a bad feeling it wouldn't be pleasant, but for some reason, it was important for me to remember. I never forgot any of my weird encounters with the ghoulies, or other strange stuff in my neighborhood. Why had I let this one slip? Had something, or someone, made me forget?

As we rolled down the highway, the pumpkin field now a faint blur in the distance, I thought long and hard about the day before. Mom had picked me up, just as she had today, and then, we'd gone to get Bradley and Logan at their school in Arroyo Grande. Once we got home, my older brothers had raced to the front door, pushing and shoving each other despite the many warnings from Mom. I had lingered behind. I always lingered behind because my brothers liked to torment me. Usually I didn't mind, but it got tiring after a while.

My sister Meggy had already come home and was downstairs in her room doing her homework. We weren't supposed to go into her room without her permission, but Logan and Bradley always did. I only went into her room without permission if it was a dire emergency, like on Saturday mornings when no one else was up, and I needed her to turn on the TV for me.

Bradley and Logan were so preoccupied with their argument over who had scored more points in basketball during lunch recess, and Mom was too busy keeping them from getting into a physical fight, that they didn't notice my sluggishness. I was okay with that. I didn't want to get stuck in the middle of it anyway, so I had dragged my feet and stared at the path leading up to our front door.

A low, grumbling complaint from a eucalyptus tree growing beside our house grabbed my attention before I could reach the front door. I forgot the uneven path and the patches of moss growing between the cracks and cast my eyes toward the sliver, sickle-shaped leaves above.

Black Bird

It didn't take long to spot the bird that had made the noise. It was a crow, at least, I thought it was a crow. A large, black smudge grasping one of the dead tree branches with its clawed feet, its red eyes trained on me. Suddenly, I felt very aware of my surroundings. I could smell the sweet, spongy scent of the swamp in the canyon behind our house. I could feel the chill of the fog rolling in off the ocean, its damp breath coating my skin. A car pulled into one of the driveways three houses down, and the distinctive crunch of tires crushing the gravelly asphalt grated against my ears. I shivered, but I was pretty sure it wasn't from the encroaching cold.

Shaking my head, I glanced back up at the black bird and found it still studying me. I narrowed my eyes. Was it really a crow? I mean, it looked just like the crows I saw flying around the neighborhood, but this one was so big, much bigger than the others. And, it had red eyes. Crows didn't have red eyes. They had black eyes. Then, something even more bizarre happened. A dense coat of smoke, deep red in color, seemed to seep through the crow's feathers, like steam rising off frost-coated roofs on cold mornings.

The giant black bird fluffed its feathers, then craned its neck forward and let out one long, low caw. If I didn't know any better, I would have sworn it said *Aiden*.

With my heart pounding in my throat, I ran to the front door. Well, I tried to run. My clumsy legs and feet refused to move as quickly as I wanted them to. It was like wading through thick mud. I pawed at the doorknob once I reached the door, frantic to get it open, so I could hide in the safety of the house. This black bird was like those ghoulies. I knew it. It had the same dark red, murky, black light glow to it that the other monsters had.

The siren of a fire engine wailing like a banshee snapped me out of my reflection. I blinked and looked up, surprised to find that I was still in the back seat of my Mom's car and not standing on the threshold of our living room. She had pulled over onto the shoulder of the road to let the fire engine pass, its bright color painting a red streak against the grey and brown faces of the distant hills to the east. As she pulled back out onto the highway, I took a few steadying breaths. The recollection of yesterday's ordeal was now fresh and bright in my mind. Wanting to recall the rest, I let my thoughts descend back into my mind, hoping to dredge up the remainder of the memory.

I must have gotten the front door open at some point because the next thing I remembered was me standing in our living room, staring into the kitchen as Mom asked Meghan to peel the potatoes while she went to get Jack and Joey from day care. Still feeling rattled from the strange bird, I had headed toward my big sister, ignoring Bradley and Logan, who had transferred their argument about who was the better basketball player to who was better at playing video games. Sometimes, I liked to watch them beat each other up while in the guise of the colorful characters on the TV screen, but not that afternoon. I wanted the comfort only my big sister could give me.

Meghan was tall, and kind and pretty. She was also a lot more quiet than my brothers, and she knew a lot of stuff. But my favorite thing about my sister was that she had the same glowing skin as me. Crinkling my nose, I held out my arm, the loose flannel sleeve slipping from my wrist and bunching up at my elbow. Usually, the pale blue glow wasn't so bright, but today it was almost the color of the TV screen when Bradley or Logan shut off their video game console. I wondered if it had anything to do with the big crow.

Shivering a little, I padded across the cold kitchen floor toward Meggy. She must not have heard me, because I had to say something to get her attention. What I wanted to say was, *Meggy, there is a weird bird outside, and it's scaring me. Can you help?* What came out was only, "Help?"

Meghan paused and glanced down at me. She smiled, her hazel eyes flashing to green, blue and then grey. That was another cool thing about Meggy. She had neat eyes. I wondered if my eyes changed, too. Sometimes, it felt like they did, but I never looked at them in the mirror. Maybe they were like the rest of me, hidden behind that one-way mirror that surrounded me.

"Sure, buddy," she answered. "Do you know where the colander is? Big yellow bowl with holes like lemons?"

Although I hadn't been asking if she needed help, I nodded anyway. I knew what she was talking about, and helping my sister might take my mind off the bird. We used the colander to drain the water from boiled noodles, or to wash off berries or salad, and it was stored below the microwave with all the other big pots and pans. The drawer was stuck a little, and it took me a while to pull it open and fish out the colander. It wasn't heavy, but my arms refused to lift it. Instead, I ended up dragging it behind me, making all kinds of noise. It was so embarrassing, never being able to do anything the way normal kids could. Meghan never seemed to notice, though. Sometimes, I imagined she could see me, the real me, but she never said so.

After taking the colander from me, Meghan got back to work washing and peeling the potatoes. My brothers continued to shoot imaginary fireballs at one another, and that icy chill still clung to my skin.

Aaaiiidennn ...

I jumped and felt my eyes grow wide and the blood drain from my face. A voice, like the crackle of dry bones snapping under heavy feet, had called my name. I spun around, wondering if Logan and Bradley had heard it.

"Die! Die you orange mutant!" Logan was hissing at the TV, as he pressed the button on his controller with the enthusiasm of a woodpecker.

Bradley only laughed, a maniacal cackle. "I don't think so! You can't get past my shield!"

No. As crazy as their conversation was, it hadn't been them who'd said my name, and clearly, they hadn't heard it.

I glanced up at Meghan. She was still peeling the potatoes. She hadn't heard it, either. The voice was in my head.

As if it read my thoughts, the voice spoke again.

Little Fae-child ... it crooned in that eerie whisper.

Faebound

This time, I didn't check to see if anyone else heard. All I wanted to do was not be scared anymore. Taking three steps forward, I flung my arms around Meghan's leg and held on tight, burying my face against her jeans right above her knee. I squeezed my eyes shut and prayed. *Please, please go away, whoever you are!*

My plea was answered with a raspy chuckle, followed by, *Hello, little Fae-child. Do you know what you are?*

It was such a cold voice, with the kind of tone that witches used in movies when they were trying to make kids think they were nice, when really they just wanted to stick you in a great big cauldron and turn you into stew.

I used to think witches and goblins and monsters were all make-believe, especially since Logan and Bradley had always try to scare me and Jack and Joey with stories about them. At first, I thought they could see the monsters too, but when they started describing what they looked like, I knew they were only teasing. If they really knew about them, they would be even more scared than me, I bet. The ghoulies didn't scare me so much anymore, since I had grown used to them, but this strange voice terrified me.

I clung to my big sister for a long time. When the voice didn't return, I stole a glance upward only to find Meggy standing unnaturally still, the potato peeler gripped tightly in one hand, her other palm pressed against the rim of the sink. Her eyes were fixed on something outside the window. Curious, I followed her gaze. What I saw then frightened me so much I gasped, letting my sister's leg go. It was the black bird, only it looked as if it had grown in size. The strange, dark red glow had grown, too, seeping from the bird like some demon fog. Long, wispy tendrils of it crawled down the trunk of the tree and over the branches, the pointed ends looking like earth worms seeking damp soil to burrow into. One of the tendrils had pulled away from the tree and was stretching toward the window.

My instincts told me to run, even as my conscience insisted I stay and guard my big sister. I took several steps back and opened my mouth, wanting to scream. I must have made some sound because

Meghan snapped out of her daze, her hands jerking up as if returning to the chore she had forgotten about. Her hands must have moved too fast because instead of peeling the potato skin, the peeler slipped and cut her knuckle.

"Crud!" Meghan hissed, dropping the peeler and clutching her hand.

"Meghan? Are you okay?"

I jumped. When did Mom get home?

"Bradley! Logan! Turn those video games off and finish the potatoes. I need to see to your sister's hand."

All around me, chaos erupted. Groaning, Logan and Bradley obeyed, shuffling into the kitchen with glum looks on their faces. Mom was pulling Meghan down the hallway toward the bathroom and Jack and Joey, recently released from the captivity of the day care center, started chasing each other around the house, screeching in delight.

As my two older brothers commenced with the potato peeling, resuming their fight, this time using soggy potato peels instead of fireballs and magical shields, I quietly snuck out of the kitchen and headed for the room I shared with the twins. Jack and Joey hardly noticed as I disappeared down the hallway, having abandoned their chase game for the toy basket kept next to the couch.

I passed the bathroom on the way, peeking in to make sure Meghan was okay. Mom was clucking like a hen while my sister tried to assure her it was only a nick. Meggy didn't see me as I passed, but she looked shaken, no matter how she tried to reassure Mom. Her skin was pale, and her eyes were shifting color faster than usual. Had she heard the voice as well? Had she seen what I'd seen?

Hoping that the horrible bird was gone now and the strange voice with it, I slipped into my room and climbed onto my bed. Although the window on the far wall looked out over the opposite side of our yard, I closed the blinds anyway. It took me a long time to get the plastic rod to twirl in the right direction, but once I could no longer see any daylight, I breathed a sigh of relief. Selecting one of my favorite comic books, one sporting a hero wearing green, I had curled up on my pillow and read until Mom called us all into the kitchen for dinner.

"Aiden, honey, did you hear me?"

I blinked and glanced up to find my mom turned in the driver's seat and giving me a worried look. We were home and parked in our driveway. When had that happened? I shook my head. No. I hadn't heard her. I had been so preoccupied with recalling the incident in the kitchen with Meggy and the weird voice that I hadn't even noticed most of the drive home, let alone what Mom had been saying.

She smiled kindly and said, "We are going to see Dr. Sellers tomorrow morning. We are going to try this medication, and if it doesn't help, you won't have to keep taking it, okay?"

Will it make me sick? Will it make me different? Will it make the creepy voice go away for good and make it so I don't see the ghoulies anymore?

Knowing none of those words would ever come out of my mouth, I simply said, "Kay."

Mom smiled and ruffled my hair, then released her seat belt and stepped out of the car. Although it had scared me, I was glad I remembered everything. If the black bird and the ghoulies were really trying to hurt me or Meghan, knowing as much about them as I could might help someday.

Not wanting to linger in the car, especially if the crow was back, I quickly unsnapped my seatbelt and climbed out onto the concrete after my mom. The car door slammed shut a little harder than I had meant it to, but I didn't let the guilt get to me. Instead, I hurried toward Mom, grabbing her hand as we walked the short distance to the house. I didn't even look into the trees. The last thing I wanted to see was that black bird staring at me with glowing red eyes again.

-Part Three-
The Green Man

Wednesday was the slowest day ever. I didn't go to school because Mom and I had the appointment with Dr. Sellers in the middle of the morning. She said that since it would take us a while to get done with the appointment, we might as well stay home. She had called the high school the day before to get a substitute teacher, so I got to spend the morning with my mom. We watched cartoons, and Mom helped me put together my Halloween costume.

Unlike Bradley and Logan, who had picked out their costumes weeks ago, and Jack and Joey, who were too young to care what they were for Halloween, I was a little more particular about what I dressed as. I never liked the costumes at the stores, so I always had Mom or Dad or Meggy help me make something. This year, I wanted to be a super hero from one of my favorite comics, but I wanted to make it a little different by adding a cape and a mask instead of a helmet. I had my old green sweatpants and sweatshirt (since green was my favorite color), and while we had been shopping for my older brothers' costumes, we had stopped by the bath aisle where I'd found a nice, big, bright green towel to use as a cape. With a little bit of glue, glitter and paint, Mom was now helping me finish up my mask.

At ten o'clock, we left for the doctor's office, my mask drying atop a paper plate on the kitchen table. Dr. Sellers was really nice, and she always gave me a sucker when we left, especially if I had to get a shot. Today, I didn't need a shot. She mostly talked to my mom and then scribbled something on her clipboard. On the way out, my mom picked up a bag from the lobby. The new medicine I was going to try.

"Dr. Sellers says you can start taking this tomorrow," she said, as we returned to the car.

I nodded somberly, my mouth too full of lime sucker to say anything.

When we got home, it was lunch time, so Mom made us some peanut butter and jelly sandwiches, and I drew and colored in my sketchbook while Mom did some work on her laptop. Later that afternoon, we had to pick up Logan, Bradley, Jack and Joey, and by the time we returned home, we were all bursting to get out of the car.

I looked for Meggy when I walked through the front door. It was after three, so she should have been home, but she was probably in her room studying. Meghan studies a lot, but most of the time I think she just likes the quiet of her bedroom. It can get pretty noisy with all us boys running around the house. Sometimes, I wish it was just her and me, and then I feel bad for wishing it. I love all my siblings, but I think I'm more like Meggy when it comes to quiet time.

The twins had scattered all of their toys over the living room floor, and Bradley and Logan were on the side of the house where the basketball hoop was attached, practicing their shots.

I padded across the carpet, sidestepping a herd of plastic triceratops and an army of small, dark green soldiers as I aimed for the sliding glass door in the kitchen.

"Outside," I said to Mom as I passed.

"Okay, honey," she responded as she chopped vegetables and tossed them into a frying pan. "Be careful. You know how competitive your brothers can get."

I nodded and with great effort, heaved the door open and then slammed it shut behind me. The only reason Mom let me go out with my older brothers alone was because she could check on us through the glass door every now and then.

Outside, the air was crisp and cool, but the sky was a clear blue above. Bradley and Logan were playing a one-on-one game, and as soon as they saw me, Logan said, "Good! You can get the ball for us when it goes out of bounds. And you can make sure it doesn't go down the hill, okay Aiden?"

I nodded and crossed the concrete, plopping down on the edge of the low retaining wall to watch them. I was perfectly happy with this task. As much as I'd love to play basketball, I knew I wasn't nearly nimble enough to be any good. Most likely, I'd trip over my own feet and cause everyone else to fall over me. Nope. Basketball wasn't my thing.

Logan dribbled past Bradley, shoving him aside and making him stumble. He sped toward the hoop, tossing the ball a little too hard. It slammed against the backboard, then bounced off the rim and headed straight for me.

"Get it, Aiden!" Logan cried.

I felt my eyes widen, and I stood, stretching my arms up as far above my head as I could. I guess I moved too slow because the ball bounced right over me and went flying down the hill onto the equestrian trail behind our house.

Both Bradley and Logan threw their heads back and groaned.

"You were supposed to stop it!" Logan pointed out.

I glared at him. Well, at least I tried to glare at him. I wanted to tell him that I had been trying to stop it.

When I continued to stand there, Bradley threw his hands up in the air. "Aiden!" he complained. "Go get the ball! It's your fault it went down there."

I looked up at my older brother, wanting very much to punch him. I didn't like it when he bossed me around. I hated it even more when he blamed things on me that I had no control over.

Logan turned to Bradley and said, "Don't be stupid. He won't be able to find it. It went too far down the trail. I'll just go get it."

Bradley made another whining sound, but I wasn't paying attention. Sure, I didn't like being bossed around or blamed for things, but neither of those was worse than people thinking I was helpless.

Screwing up my face and mustering all the energy and concentration I could, I shouted, "No!" then, "Get ball."

Faebound

Without waiting for my brothers to consider what I had said, I spun on my heel and crawled through the fence, almost tripping over the plants growing on the small slope that led down to the trail. I would show both of them I could do something as simple as find a lost basketball.

Plucking dead leaves and tiny, broken twigs from my hair and clothes, I stumbled out onto the wide dirt path. The local horse owners used this trail a lot, so the sand was soft and deep in some places. And there were 'road apples' everywhere. That's what Bradley and Logan called the horse poop. They thought it was so hilarious, and sometimes, they threatened to throw them at me when I didn't do what they asked. Fortunately, I stayed inside most of the time. Having big brothers was such a pain.

Sidestepping a nearby pile of road apples, I headed farther down the trail, following the large, basketball-shaped divots in the sand until I spotted a small groove that indicated which direction the ball had rolled. And my brothers thought I was an idiot. I bet they didn't know how to track a basketball.

I took my time locating the ball, mostly to get back at my brothers for being rude. It wasn't hard, since it was so nice down in this canyon, what with the tall eucalyptus trees creating plenty of shade, their sickle-shaped leaves rustling in the breeze far above my head. On the left side of the trail, the hillside fell away about fifty feet down into the swamp below. Small shrubs and young trees dotted the slope and made it pretty much impossible for anyone to cross, unless they wanted to end up full of blackberry thorns and stinging nettle welts.

Fortunately, I spotted the basketball only a few more yards down the path. It had rolled pretty far, almost halfway down to where the trail curved to the left to cross the shallowest part of the swamp. I was glad I didn't have to go down that far. The tree branches curved overhead and made it dark and spooky, and it just didn't feel right even from far away.

I stepped onto the dead grass tangled along the side of the trail, zeroing in on the ball, its bright orange color standing out like a disregarded safety vest. The basketball had wedged itself between a tree stump and a pile of dead brush someone had piled up to make a fort. It was a few feet from the path, and I had to climb through the shrubs a little to reach it.

Placing my foot on a large branch, I leaned forward, my tongue sticking out of the side of my mouth and my fingers stretching toward the ball. I heard the crack before I felt my weight give out underneath me. The branch, which had looked sturdy, was really rotten in the center. I pitched forward, the ball breaking loose as well, and the both of us crashed halfway down the hill. I landed in a small clump of overgrown shrubs beneath a willow tree, the ball stuck between me and the ground. I tried moving, but my ankle hurt, and something sharp dug into my shoulder. Taking a careful glance to the side, I realized the pain was caused by a blackberry branch that had come loose from the main plant several feet away.

As I lay there, I reflected in silent misery on how I'd been so proud of myself for being smarter than my brothers. Now, I was hoping they'd come looking for me soon. I tried getting up, but my ankle twinged a little, and I rolled back onto my side.

Just when I was about to give up and start screaming to get Bradley and Logan's attention, I heard something rustling in the reeds somewhere in front of me. I rolled over again, trying not to make my ankle worse, and blinked out over the swamp. Most of the marsh was clogged up with reeds and cattails, with only a few pools of blackish water visible from what I could see. A small patch of the plants had been shoved aside and smashed flat, giving me a clear view of the shore on the other side.

The opposite shore was littered with dead, brown eucalyptus leaves, the trees from which they'd fallen spread out just enough to create a meadow of sorts. A clump of poison oak, the leaves going red for the autumn, crawled up each of the trunks of the trees like scarlet lace. Beyond the meadow were more trees and shrubs growing thick and crowding the side of another slope.

Faebound

As I studied the view, that rustling sound from earlier returned, this time accompanied by a strange growling. Immediately, I became completely still, not daring to even breathe or blink. I knew that sound. Whatever was moving on the opposite shore was a ghoulie. Would it see me stuck under the tree? Would it try to come after me this time, now that I was helpless?

Before I could think much more about it, the ghoulie pushed free of the reeds and scurried up onto the dry land, shaking itself like a wet dog. I didn't see why it would. It's not like it had any fur to keep dry. Instead, a scattering of coarse hairs, like those on a pig, stuck out from a hide that looked to be the same shade and consistency as dried tar. It had a long snout complete with bright white, pointed teeth that didn't fit all the way into its mouth, and a tail as long and thin as one of the reeds growing in the mire.

The ghoulie had pulled something out of the water and was now pinning it down with clawed feet and tearing at it with its teeth. I narrowed my eyes, but the only thing I noticed about the object was that it was red and brown. Some small animal, most likely.

Just when I was certain the ghoulie would finish its meal and move on, another one came charging out of nowhere, slamming into the first with enough force to knock it off its feet. The first ghoulie tumbled into a patch of poison oak, the dead animal still clutched in its teeth as the other readied itself for another attack. The creatures were a good thirty yards or so away, and blocked somewhat by the water and the reeds, but I wanted to get out of there as soon as I could, just in case they smelled me or sensed me somehow. I jiggled my foot experimentally and was relieved to find the pain in my ankle wasn't nearly as severe as it had been ten minutes ago. Maybe I hadn't sprained it after all.

Before I could roll over and start climbing back up the hill, something unexpected happened. As the two ghoulies circled one another in a game of tug-of-war with the dead thing, a long, thin object came darting through the air and lodged itself into the first creature. The monster screeched, the sound a combination of hard chalk grating against a blackboard and a rabbit screaming. I ground my teeth together as goose pimples popped up all over my skin. Another one of those long sticks came flying from the right, and I realized what they were: arrows. The second arrow struck the other ghoulie in the face, and as it added its own cry of pain, it turned its head in my direction. I felt my face pale and my stomach turn over. The arrow was sticking out of the monster's sunken eye, the flesh smoking where the arrow shaft touched it. It staggered for a moment longer, then collapsed to the ground.

Some more rustling on the slope announced something else approaching. Oh no. Were there more ghoulies out here? Instead of an entire herd of monsters, a huge white dog burst free of the brush on the other side of the meadow, coming to a stop next to the dying ghoulie. I gaped in complete surprise. He was big enough for me to ride, if he was my dog, and he was all snowy white except for his ears. They looked like they were dark red or brown.

Just when I thought I couldn't get any more surprises today, the branches of the far oak tree parted and someone stepped out into the meadow. It was a man, I think, because he wore dark green pants and a long, olive green trench coat, the kind guys in the army sometimes wear. The coat was hooded, and the man had the hood pulled over his head, so I couldn't see his face at first. In one hand, he carried a bow, almost as tall as he was, and there was a sack of arrows flung across his back. He approached the meadow cautiously, his boots making barely any noise against the leaf litter and fallen branches. When he came within ten feet of the dead ghoulies, he held up a hand and the dog walked over to his side. The gloves he wore were the same color as the jacket, and the fingertips had been cut off.

I swallowed hard. Maybe he was one of the strangers Mom and Dad had warned me about. They told me that some people lived away from others, and that some of these people were dangerous. They had always told me that I should assume they were all dangerous, just to be safe. I scrunched up my nose, trying to decide whether this stranger was dangerous or not.

Faebound

After scratching the dog behind the ears, he moved closer to the ghoulies and got down on one knee. I wanted to shout out and warn him that the ghoulies were not natural, and they might still hurt him even if they were dead. But then, an even more profound thought occurred to me: Only I could see the ghoulies. If he had shot them and was now looking at them, he could see them, too.

The man reached out and pulled one, then the other, arrow from the dead monsters. He wiped the arrow tips on the ground. Then, without even looking, returned them to the quiver on his back. As he started to stand, he reached up and pushed the hood back from his face. I couldn't really see it from where I hid under the bushes, but his hair looked dark, and he was really tall. Taller than Dad. Taller even than Kevin, our neighbor down the street who played basketball for the high school where Mom worked. He was bigger, too, almost like a Viking from one of Bradley's warrior encyclopedia books. I couldn't see his eyes at all, even when he turned his head as if to survey his surroundings. Panicking a little, I buried my face in the leaves, inhaling dust and the scent of damp mildew. My heart was thundering in my ears, and my ankle began to ache a little. Had he seen me? I hoped he hadn't. I was wearing Bradley's old camouflage zip-up sweatshirt, but something about this stranger told me he might be able to see me even if I had buried myself under all the leaves.

Eventually, I heard a light whistle and the sound of movement across the water. Gathering up my courage, I lifted my head just enough to peek out with one eye. The stranger and his white dog were gone, and where the ghoulies used to be, there were only two black piles of ash.

Before he got the chance to come back, I squirmed around until my head faced uphill once again and, using one arm to push the basketball ahead of me, I crawled back up the hill. Once out on the horse trail again, I spun around, wincing a little because of my sore ankle. It didn't hurt that bad, but it still bothered me a little. Besides my ankle, the tops of my hands were a little scratched from the blackberry vines, but at least I hadn't fallen into a patch of poison oak or stinging nettles.

"Aiden!" I heard someone call out.

I jumped nearly five feet, my heart staying airborne even when I landed back onto solid ground.

"Aiden, let's go! It's almost dinner time, and you know Mom's gonna make us do homework after!"

It was just Logan and Bradley, finally looking to see what had happened to me. There was no way I could tell them, even if I wanted to, about what I had seen and heard. They would just assume I had tripped and fallen, like I sometimes do. As much as I hated the way my autism often made me slow to react and unable to talk clearly, in situations like this, it was probably for the best.

I finished brushing off the dead leaves and sticky, moldy dirt and scooped up the basketball. Without glancing back down at the swamp, I turned toward home, praying that there were no more ghoulies and no more strangers with huge dogs.

Yet, while I hurried back up the trail, the events of the last several minutes spun around in my mind like a colorful pinwheel in the wind. Who had that man been, and why was he able to see the ghoulies? Where had he come from? I had never seen him in our neighborhood before, and I was good at noticing new people.

As I turned to climb up the slope leading into our back yard, I thought about one more thing that unnerved me about the Green Man, something I hadn't even noticed at first because he was all covered up by that coat. When he had pulled his hood back to look at the ghoulies, his skin had been glowing, just like mine and Meggy's.

-Part Four-

Corpse Hounds

Bradley and Logan were sitting on the fence when I got back from fetching the basketball. It wasn't a real fence, just part of one that marked the edge of the yard. I didn't climb on it too much because it was made out of split rails, and it was full of splinters. Logan was sitting on the top rail facing the swamp, while Bradley was on the side that ran parallel with the horse trail, throwing rocks down into the overgrown canyon below. I could hear the rocks crashing into the underbrush, and when a covey of quail was startled into taking flight, I almost jumped out of my skin. I had a feeling anything I noticed moving down in the swamp for the next several weeks would spook me.

"There you are!" Logan exclaimed. "What have you been doing all this time?"

He hopped down from the railing and crossed his arms. He was the oldest of my brothers, and therefore, thought he was in charge of the rest of us. Logan lifted one eyebrow, doing a perfect imitation of Mom when she wanted answers.

"Who cares!" Bradley whined. "Just give us the basketball already. Mom will be calling us in for dinner any minute."

My other brother jumped down from the fence and came toward me, swiping the ball out of my hands. He could have it. That basketball brought nothing but trouble.

"You coming, Logan?" Bradley asked as he climbed back over the fence.

Logan didn't answer right away. He was looking at me funny.

"Logan!" Bradley barked, making to throw the ball at him.

"Hang on!" Logan bit back, holding up a hand, his eyes still fixed on me.

Did I have dirt on my face? Had I torn my pants or shirt?

I tried not to feel self-conscious, but I failed miserably. Finally, I couldn't take it anymore, and I dropped my eyes to the dirt below. I shoved my hands into my pockets, wincing a little as the rough fabric rubbed against the scratches on my skin.

"What happened, Aiden?" Logan finally said, concern overriding the haughty tone of his voice. "You've got scratches all over you. And mud. Did you go down to the swamp?"

I looked back up at him, his blue eyes serious. Okay. So maybe Logan wasn't all that bad, for a brother. He might be a jerk to me most of the time, but if anyone outside of our family ever tried to make me feel bad, or if I was hurt, he was the first one, besides Mom and Meggy, to make sure I was okay.

Apparently, Bradley couldn't take the delay any longer. Sighing dramatically, he tossed the ball at the hoop and turned back toward us, not even bothering to see if he made the shot. The ball bounced off the rim and fell back to earth, rolling out into the middle of the lawn before coming to a stop. He squeezed between the two rails of the fence, half stumbling down the short slope and coming to a skidding halt on the horse path.

"Dude. Looks like you got dragged through the woods by a pack of coyotes."

I stiffened. Did I really look that bad? At least my ankle had stopped hurting. Both my brothers were staring at me now, so I cast my eyes downward again, pushing around the loose dirt on the ground with my shoe. The scene from the meadow across the shallow part of the swamp kept coming back to me: the ugly ghoulies, the white dog, the stranger in the green army trench coat with the bow and arrows and glowing skin.

Taking a shallow breath and letting it out quickly, I opened my mouth and said simply, "Fell down."

"I'll say," Bradley commented sarcastically. "Fell down the hill and rolled all the way to the bottom."

Logan stepped forward, nudging Bradley out of the way. "Did you fall into a patch of blackberry bushes?"

I nodded. Technically, I hadn't, but agreeing with their assumptions was easier than trying to tell them the truth. There were two things wrong with that. First, they wouldn't believe me even if I could tell them the truth, and secondly, it was physically impossible for me to do that.

"Better get you inside and show Mom," Logan said, taking charge in his big brotherly way.

He draped an arm over my shoulder and started leading me back up to the house, Bradley trailing behind grumbling about missing out on playing basketball. Despite my nervousness about the ghoulies and the strange green man, a warm feeling welled up from somewhere near my heart and spread out to my fingers and toes. Suddenly, I didn't feel so scared anymore because I had a big brother to look out for me. Usually, I only hugged Meggy or Mom or Dad, but as we walked back into the house, I reached out my hand and grabbed onto the hem of Logan's shirt. Okay, it wasn't really a hug, but when I glanced up at my brother's face, it looked like he was smiling just a little. I did my best to return the expression.

The look on Mom's face when we stepped back into the kitchen was one of horror.

"Aiden! What on earth happened to you?"

"The basketball rolled down the horse trail, and Aiden went to go get it," Bradley offered, his innocent tone spiced with just a pinch of guilt.

Bradley had mastered the art of appearing angelic when faced with possible punishment.

"By himself?" Mom asked, her voice hardening.

She stood there like an angry hen, her fists pressed against her hips, a dish towel hanging from one of them.

Corpse Hounds

I scowled. Well, I tried to scowl. I couldn't tell if it was actually working. I understood that Mom was extra protective over me because of my autism, but I should be able to go after a stray basketball without someone accompanying me and holding my hand the entire way. And then, the images of the ghoulies flashed into my mind, and I bit my lip, dropping my eyes. Okay, maybe I shouldn't go wandering down into the swamp by myself, even with my brothers a few dozen yards away.

"He didn't go very far, and we were watching him from the fence the whole time," Logan insisted.

That wasn't entirely true. If they had been, they would have seen me fall and would have come after me.

"I don't care," Mom said, straightening back up and reaching out to take my hand. "Who knows what's down there. People used to dump their trash in that culvert all the time before the Land Conservancy got involved and cleaned it up. There might still be some residual toxins in the soil or rusty shards of metal hidden under the bushes."

Mom threw the towel over her shoulder with her free hand and started tugging me down the hallway to the bathroom. She lifted me up onto the counter and ran warm water in the sink, then pulled out some hydrogen peroxide, bandages and antibiotic ointment. She cleaned my cuts with warm water, pouring hydrogen peroxide over them just to be safe, then patted them dry and added the ointment and bandages to the bad ones. There were only a few since most of the scrapes had been shallow ones from the blackberry brambles.

After patching me up and wiping away all the dirt, she took me to my room and helped me change into a clean set of clothes, grumbling the entire time about how I shouldn't wander off by myself or let my older brothers boss me around. I simply stood there in silence as Mom tugged on a clean T-shirt and a fresh pair of sweatpants. It was embarrassing having your mom dress you when you were seven, but dinner would be ready soon, and unless I had a half an hour to get through the ordeal by myself, someone had to help me. Pushing buttons into buttonholes and tying shoes were especially hard for me, so most of my pants had elastic bands, and my shoes fastened using Velcro.

By the time we returned to the living room, Dad was home and checking on the dinner. When he turned to Mom to ask about it, he took one look at the expression on her face and clamped his mouth shut.

"Dinner will be ready in ten minutes," she snapped. "You can wait that long, or better yet, next time you can be the one to make it for all of us."

Dad backed away with his hands raised. "I was just going to stir the vegetables in the pan. The boys said Aiden had fallen down outside." He cast me a quick look, probably checking for more deadly injuries than the scrapes that were now covered in bandages. "Are you okay, Aiden?"

I nodded my head vigorously. I was fine. If anything was wrong with me at all, it had nothing to do with the physical injuries, but everything to do with the mental ones from all the ghoulie sightings in the past few days.

Once everyone was convinced that I wasn't going to drop dead anytime soon, we started getting the table ready for dinner. Mom sent Logan to tell Meghan dinner was ready, and Dad was getting the twins latched into their high chairs. To my great relief, dinner went on like it always did with Bradley telling us all about school. Apparently, one of the girls in Logan's class had a crush on him and was always following him around the playground. Upon hearing this, Logan turned bright red and tried to jab Bradley with his fork.

Dad quickly diffused the situation, and Logan retaliated by informing Bradley that having a girl like him was better than having all the girls in his class avoid him because he still picked his nose, at which time Mom stepped in with a quick lecture about what was appropriate to talk about at the dinner table. Jack and Joey didn't have much to say, considering they were still practically babies, but they laughed and seemed to enjoy everyone else's conversation.

Corpse Hounds

While all this was going on, I slid my eyes in my sister's direction. Meghan was being quiet, more so than usual, only picking at her food and eating very little of it. I felt my stomach clench with unease. Her eyes were distant, and her skin wasn't glowing as much as it usually did. Now I would have Meggy to worry about on top of everything else.

After dinner, Dad helped Mom get the twins ready for bed while Bradley and Logan reluctantly started their homework. Meggy disappeared into her room. She probably had to study, too. High school had lots of homework, she had told me once. I decided to head to my room. I didn't feel like coloring while my brothers worked at the table, and we weren't allowed to have the TV on if anyone was studying. Instead, I curled up in my bed and read one of my chapter books. After a while, I set it aside and turned off my lamp.

It took me a long time to fall asleep that night, what with my own busy thoughts and the garbled, sleeping sounds floating over from my twin brothers' side of the room. Eventually, I drifted off, the undulating shadows cast by Jack and Joey's fish tank filling up the room like dancing demons. When I opened my eyes again, I was lying on my back, the brilliant sunlight filtering through the canopy of bright green leaves above. I squinted, and lifted up a hand to rub at my eyes. To my surprise, I wasn't clumsy or slow about it.

Taking a breath, I rolled over and got up onto my knees, surveying this unfamiliar place I'd found myself in. Tall eucalyptus trees surrounded a meadow carpeted with brown leaves and small patches of poison ivy. To my left was what appeared to be a stream bed, choked with long, lanky stems of reeds and cattails. A cool breeze shifted the silvery green, sickle-shaped leaves above, and beyond the snaking river of emerald bog plants was the slope of a hillside covered in oak and more eucalyptus. I swallowed, my mouth dry and tasting like dust. I knew this place. I was in the swamp behind my house. In the very meadow where I'd seen the Green Man kill the ghoulies.

Suddenly, my skin prickled with anxiety, and the faint blue glow to my skin intensified. Were there more ghoulies around? Why was I here? I should have been asleep in bed, safe inside my house.

Before I could contemplate anything more, a low, rattling growl froze the blood in my veins. I stayed absolutely still, my heart galloping like a race horse.

The growl was joined by another one, and the snapping of twigs and rustling of brush answered my question. Yes. There were more ghoulies around.

Slowly, I turned my head. I shouldn't have. Three monsters, all close to the size of that white dog I'd seen the other day, emerged from the shadows cast by the brush-clogged edge of the meadow. They were so much bigger and so much more terrifying than the other ghoulies I'd seen before. They were bone-thin, like greyhounds that had starved to death and then been buried for a few weeks. The breeze picked up again, this time blowing in my direction, and their smell hit my nose like a slap: dead animal flesh, mixed with rotting eggs and scorched hair. The ghoulie closest to me peeled back its mud-black lips and snarled. Long, wicked yellow teeth lined its jaws, and deep within its throat, a fire burned, like the throat of a dragon I'd seen in a movie once.

I gagged in reaction to their stench and forced down a sob, then stood all the way up, intending to run. But then, I realized I couldn't run. I had a hard enough time keeping my feet in front of me while I walked.

One of the rotting hounds threw back its head and bayed, a long, low call that brought to mind images of battle fields and loved ones wailing over mass graves. I cried out and turned, not caring that I wouldn't make it very far. I had to get away from these things, even if the only way to escape meant dying once they tore me to shreds.

To my utter surprise, my feet obeyed my mind, and I went tearing across the meadow, intending to head toward the place where I could cross the swamp. I didn't make it very far before one of the ghoulies leapt forward, coming to land to my right. It snapped at me, and I screamed, changing directions. Another one was right behind me, and the third somewhere on my left. I ran in the only direction I had left: straight ahead and deeper into the woods. I only hoped that I'd find a tree I could climb as I made my escape.

Cold sweat poured down my back, and my lungs burned as I pushed myself, faster, farther, as the three ghoulies chased after me. Their howls sent goose bumps all over my skin and made my heart skip a beat, but I kept running, leaping over fallen logs and sliding down small slopes covered in leaves. At some point, I stumbled out onto another trail. If I turned right, I could head out to the road that dead ended before reaching the crossing point over the swamp. That was my better option. Taking a few deep breaths, I turned in that direction, only to have one of the ghoulies bound up onto the trail, its black claws skidding against the packed dirt.

I cried out again and pulled up short, nearly tripping this time. Never in my life had I been able to run so well or so fast. The monster growled at me, panting. A half-rotten tongue lolled from its mouth, and the fire in its throat flared in time with its breathing.

The other two were on the slope above the road, eyeing me carefully. They weren't going to let me go out to the road. Whimpering and trying hard to keep the tears in my eyes from falling, I turned left and started sprinting down the trail. The ghoulies followed, herding me like a sheep. The road curved sharply to the left, and then, I could see the bottom of the culvert. It was dry this far back, but I could clearly see where the water might run through in the rainy season. I hit the sand, desperately searching around for a new direction to turn.

On the opposite side, the trail picked up and continued to wind through the eucalyptus trees. To my left, the wide, sandy canyon floor continued on, only blocked by the occasional fallen tree or patch of willows. To my right, the walls of the small canyon rose up on either side, the passage blocked by a crisscrossing of dead eucalyptus trees which had fallen into the culvert over the years. It reminded me of a pathway into a haunted mountain in one of my brothers' video games.

A cold, unnatural gust of air rolled down the canyon, freezing my sweat-slicked skin. There was no way I was going to go down that way.

Making up my mind to head back toward the place where I started, I turned left. Before I could so much as take a first step, one of the ghoulies jumped in front of me, snarling and flicking its whip-like tail. I tried to dart around it. Maybe I could lose them if I ran off-trail. My attempt at escape failed again when a second monster blocked my way. The third one joined in, and they had me cornered. I could either run directly at them, or turn and run up the culvert.

"No!" I rasped, the tears now streaming freely down my face. "No!"

They paced toward me, snapping at me when I didn't move. I took a step back, then another. They sped up. Swallowing my paralyzing fear, I turned and bolted up the canyon.

It's just your fear, Aiden, I told myself as I wove between the eucalyptus trunks. *Just your fear. You must overcome it.*

The walls of the canyon drew closer together, and the angle of the dead trees became more steep. Ahead of me, the dirt path became an eroded wall. I had come to the end. I turned around to face the ghoulies - to face my fate - but something to my right caught my eye. To my utter surprise, there was some sort of cave in the side of the canyon wall, its black throat yawning wide. Tendrils of roots and strips of dead eucalyptus bark dangled from the lip of the cave like a gruesome bead curtain hanging from a doorway.

Before I could ponder it much further, another icy gust of air poured from the hole, along with the bone-chilling clack of dry bones striking together and the squirming sound of maggots roiling in rotten meat.

The bile in my stomach rose. Something was coming. Something so terrifying, I could feel it with my instincts alone. Behind me, the rotten hounds grew restless, their growls turning to yips, but before me the black cavern seemed to yawn wider, drawing back as if it was about to spit something awful from its depths. The hideous sounds grew louder and the air colder. The wind stirred my hair, and all I could do was stand there, frozen in fear, with my fists clenched at my sides.

Before I even got a chance to see the hellish thing that was coming to kill me, everything went blank.

-Part Five-

Super Powers

I woke up, screaming at the top of my lungs. Only, there wasn't a sound escaping my throat. The screams existed only in my nightmare, and in the real world, I only lie with my eyes wide open, gasping for air.

I kicked at my bed sheets, almost descending into panic when I couldn't break free. The blankets had become twisted around me like a straight jacket. Somehow, I managed to free myself and roll over in bed, curling up into a ball. I was shaking, and cold sweat coated my skin. My eyes darted around the room, seeking out the dark corners made darker by the eerie light cast by Jack and Joey's fish tank. I expected ghoulies to come leaping out of the closet or from behind the dresser or from under my bed. Gradually, my breathing slowed along with my heart rate, and the acrid fear of the dream fizzled out with it. The grey light of dawn was just beginning to peek through the blinds, and I could hear Logan and Bradley, speaking in what they thought were whispers, arguing from their room.

Glad of the distraction, I crawled out of bed and snuck down the hallway, pushing their door open without even bothering to knock.

They both stopped their discussion and turned to look at me, Bradley scowling as usual.

"Haven't you ever heard of knocking?" Logan hissed.

Apparently, his brotherly concern from yesterday was all gone. I shrugged and said, "Loud."

Bradley turned his nasty look onto our other brother. "I told you you were making too much noise!"

"Me?!" Logan replied in exasperation.

And then, they started arguing again. Figuring I was safe for the moment, I scuttled over to get a closer look at what they had piled up in the middle of their room. A few small cans of what might have been spray paint, some random Halloween decorations, lots of candy and a large, hand-made card. That's when it dawned upon me. Today was Halloween and Meghan's birthday. They were getting ready to surprise her. If anything good ever came out of Halloween, it was that Meggy was born on this day. Smiling and deciding I was going to help, I knelt onto the ground and pulled the card toward me. My brothers had snatched it away earlier that week before I could finish the picture I was drawing.

"Aiden!" Logan complained.

"Let him finish! We need to wrap the candy anyway. Meghan will be up soon."

For the next several minutes, we worked in relative silence, only the occasional disagreement rising up between my brothers every now and again. At some point in time, the door cracked open and Mom poked her head in.

"Oh, there you are! I've started the breakfast, so be ready to go get your sister in fifteen minutes or so."

We worked for ten more minutes, Bradley and Logan doing a passable job of wrapping up the candy they'd picked out and me cleaning up the crayons and markers. When we finally spilled out into the hallway, we were greeted with the delightful smell of French toast. I breathed in deeply and smiled. The nightmare from before was already a dim memory, and I couldn't wait to wish my sister a happy birthday.

Dad was busy getting the twins fastened into their high chairs, and Mom had started depositing freshly cooked slices of French toast onto a waiting plate. Strings of black plastic cut-out bats and orange jack-o-lanterns hung between the cabinets, and Mom had to duck so she wouldn't become entangled in them. Ghosts made of white tissue paper wrapped around lollipops dangled from the chandelier above the dining room table, one of them missing a googly eye.

Faebound

"Logan, go yell downstairs for your sister," Mom said as she slid one final piece of toast onto the others.

Logan darted across the living room, and Bradley started shaking the can he held in his hand. Silly string, I realized, not spray paint. When Logan was done yelling at Meghan, he replaced the trap door that marked the entrance to her basement room and then nodded in Bradley's direction. Bradley took that as a sign and quickly made his way to the other side of Meghan's door, tossing a can of silly string to Logan on the way.

Before Meggy even reached the top of the stairs, Bradley and Logan pulled the trap door open, and she emerged, blinking in surprise at all the decorations. Two seconds later, she was ambushed by my brothers, silly string flying everywhere.

"Logan!" Meghan complained, "You totally set me up for that!"

She didn't seem too annoyed, however, because she was smiling even as she picked the sticky mess of black and orange from her hair and clothes. I managed to weave my way through the chaos, walking up to Meggy and throwing my arms around her legs. She was so tall I could never give her a real hug, not unless she was sitting on the couch with me. She placed her hand on the back of my head, and for a few seconds, I let the comforting presence of my sister flood over me. Tonight, we would go trick-or-treating, and I would have given anything to have Meggy go with us, but she was going to a school dance with her friends. I would just have to be brave.

After breakfast, Dad left for work, and Mom got the rest of us ready for the day. She dropped the twins off at the daycare down the street before taking Bradley and Logan to school. As we pulled into the drop off area of their school, I pressed my face up against the cold glass and gazed out across the parking lot. Kids dressed as zombies, fairies, witches and superheroes made their way into class. I was wearing my costume as well, but it wasn't nearly as fancy as some of the ones I was studying at the moment.

"See you after school!" Mom called out to my brothers before pulling out onto the main road.

After that, she brought me to my school, kissing me goodbye and telling me she'd be back later to pick me up. I entered the classroom to find my classmates in the Halloween spirit as well. Mrs. Warren and Miss Rodriguez were dressed up as a cat and mouse. Maddie and Bella were wearing princess costumes, and Mira looked like an over-sized teddy bear. Jake and Russell were dressed as the same superhero, one from a popular cartoon and not featured in the comic books I read. We didn't do much that day besides play games, watch a movie and have a small party before our moms and dads picked us up.

I was ready to go home, even though going home meant trick-or-treating later. Everyone was always trying to make Halloween fun for kids, as if the holiday didn't really hide creepy things in the shadows. I knew better. There were no friendly ghosts or sad monsters who just wanted to be your friend. The ghoulies were real, and they would hurt you if they got the chance.

Once Mom had made all the stops to pick up my brothers, we headed home. We had an early dinner and then waited for Dad to get home. Bradley and Logan couldn't keep still, and they started chasing each other around the living room. They looked a little ridiculous, especially Logan who had a hard time getting away from Bradley in his bulky cheeseburger costume. Dad showed up ten minutes later, begging us to give him a half an hour of peace before he took us out trick-or-treating. I felt my stomach tense up. Thirty short minutes from now, I would be going out into the dark world where the ghoulies waited for me, and maybe even those really big scary ones I'd seen in my dream.

"Zap!" Bradley screeched, jumping out from behind the couch, his over-sized alien eyes looking demonic. He had a fake laser gun pointed at me, the light on the end flashing red.

When my heartbeat returned to normal, I took a step back, holding up my hands. Best to play along.

"I'll save you, Aiden!" Logan bellowed, jumping from the back of the couch and crashing into Bradley.

My brothers collapsed in a pile of sesame seed bun and shiny green alien skin. In the next second, Dad was yelling at them to stop rough housing, and I took the opportunity to make my escape. I glanced across the living room only to see Meghan heading toward the door. She was dressed like a butterfly and wore a black dress for the dance. Part of me wanted to rush toward her and beg her to change her mind; to convince her to go trick-or-treating with us, but she was already closing the door behind her. I would have to make it on my own.

"Alright, that's it!" Dad proclaimed. "I'm going to go change, and then, we'll get going."

Ten minutes later, Dad came striding down the hallway dressed as the Grim Reaper.

"Ready boys?" he asked in a fake, spooky voice.

"Yeah!" everyone but me exclaimed.

Mom helped Dad with the twins. They were a pair of sock monkeys, and their tails were long enough for Dad to keep wrapped around his hand. I thought it was pretty funny. So did Bradley and Logan. But since Mom insisted on staying home, Dad insisted on these little tricks to keep an eye on all us boys, especially on Halloween night. If that meant treating my rowdy twin brothers like a pair of hyper puppies on leashes, then so be it.

Finally, everyone was gathered with their bags for collecting treats, and Mom was shooing us along. She didn't like us to be out too late, so the sooner we left, the sooner we could come home. I was happy with that.

By the time we were all outside and making our way down the street, the sun had just set, and twilight was staining the sky indigo and ink-blue. Bradley and Logan ran ahead of us, continuing their mock battle from inside, and although Jack and Joey tried to join them, Dad's tight hold on their tails kept them always within reach.

"I don't think so, you two," he said through the black screen taking up the front of his hood.

I opted to stick as close to Dad as possible, gripping a section of his black cloak in my fist. As we made our way down the block, I watched the shrubs along the side of the road and the bushes clogging people's yards. For a while, nothing out of the ordinary stirred in the dark.

Each house on our street had a long driveway, and the homeowners had done a good job of creating a spooky atmosphere by stringing fake spider webs everywhere or wedging foam headstones into their lawns. Spooky music floated from cracked windows, and jack-o-lanterns stood guard on front porches, the yellow candle flames in their throats flickering and making them look as if they were laughing silently at us kids as we scuttled past in slight fear.

If I didn't know the truth behind Halloween, that it was the one day of the year the ghoulies came out in hordes, I would have loved it all. Despite that fact, however, I had yet to see a single ghoulie. Just as we rounded the corner of our street and headed out onto the wider road toward the next block, I noticed something odd. In the distance, I could see the tops of the trees that clogged the swamp behind our house. I had to blink several times to clear my vision, thinking maybe I was seeing things. But I wasn't. A strange red haze was rising up from the depths of the swamp, like the weird glow I'd seen surrounding the ghoulies. Immediately, my skin began to prickle.

"Bradley, Logan! Let's go. We still have three more streets to hit before turning back," Dad called out to my brothers, snapping me back to reality.

Shivering, I moved closer to him and the twins. Something wasn't right about that strange mist. Five houses later, and we had moved closer to the swamp once again. Bradley and Logan ran down the pathway of the next house, Jack and Joey close behind. I stayed right where I was. There was a gap between this house and the next one, and I could almost see down into the bog through the space.

"Don't you want anymore candy?" Dad asked me.

Faebound

I shook my head. My bag was half full, and that would last me long enough.

"Alright, you can wait with me here then," Dad replied, putting his arm around me and pulling me close.

For a few moments, I enjoyed the comfort of being nestled up next to Dad. But when he released me, I inched closer to the edge of the road so I could see down into the swamp. What I noticed next made my stomach turn. The red mist had grown thicker and rose higher, almost as tall as me now, and I could see things churning along the edge of it: ghoulies.

"Dude! That lady gave us whole candy bars!"

Logan's voice made me jump, and I hurried back next to Dad.

Before long, we were moving once again, visiting two more houses before finishing up with the cul-de-sac. We were halfway done with our night. I could do this. I could make it through without letting the ghoulies get the better of me.

I spotted the first monster on our way down the next street. It was as big as a house cat with long, batwing ears that looked half-rotted and long, yellow teeth that did not fit in its mouth. Its dark skin hung from a bony body, and it limped as it walked. I grabbed Dad's hand and held on tight, reaching for a long eucalyptus branch protruding from a pile of yard clippings on the dirt shoulder of the road.

"Are you okay, Aiden?" Dad asked, turning to look at me.

I nodded and proceeded to use the branch as a walking stick. After that, the streets practically crawled with the horrible little monsters. Some resembled squirrels, others small dogs and raccoons. They darted back and forth between the thicker landscaping of the yards, crossing the street like rats chased out into the open. They mostly avoided the other kids in costume and their parents, and I felt myself cringing every time one came close to getting stepped on, or moved in to sniff at the hem of someone's costume. I had never seen so many ghoulies before, even during past Halloweens.

As the night dragged on, more and more of the nasty things came out of the shadows like spiders hatching from an egg sac. The soft glow of the street lamps cast them in tones of peach and orange, and I could hear their low growls as they fought with one another under the cover of darkness.

"Last street, boys!" Dad called out, tugging on the tails of my brothers and rounding Bradley and Logan up with his scythe.

"Oh, come on Dad!" Bradley groaned. "Can't we stay out a little later tonight?"

"Nope. We've been out long enough, and something's got your little brother spooked."

I blinked up at Dad in surprise. I couldn't see his expression, but I could tell he was trying to study me through his mesh mask. He couldn't see the ghoulies. No one could but me. Yet, he knew something was bothering me. Feeling relieved, I scooted closer to him and wrapped my arms around his leg, burying my face in his cloak.

Logan and Bradley groaned again and shot me acidic looks, but I didn't care. No one could see the ghoulies, and so far, they hadn't hurt anyone, but that didn't mean they wouldn't. The sooner we got home and were safe inside our house, the better.

We were lucky for most of the next street, but as we turned the corner to start making our way back up our own road, the old dog that lived across the street from Tully's house started barking wildly. I glanced up as Dad moved us across the street and blanched. The dog was surrounded by a pack of ghoulies, their ugly teeth bared and their skinny tails snapping back and forth. I remembered the dog's owner calling him Bruno once, and I knew he was blind in one eye.

"Come on, boys. He'll stop barking once we get past him," Dad reassured us.

I knew better. He wasn't just barking, but whining as well. The ghoulies were moving in closer, and a few of them darted in to bite him on the heels. He yelped and flattened his ears to his head. My heart tightened, and I stopped walking, staring across the dark street at the old dog. Although the front yard wasn't fenced, Bruno always stayed in the yard. Right now, I wished there was a fence. A fence might have kept the ghoulies out.

One of the small monsters shrunk down on its haunches and then launched itself at the dog, landing on his back and sinking its teeth into his fur. Bruno yelped again, his tail tucked between his legs.

Without even thinking, I moved, running across the street as fast as my feet would take me. I wasn't able to move as quickly or as gracefully as I had in my dream, but before I knew it I was on the lawn. What I planned to do I had no idea. All I knew was that a rage had begun boiling inside me. I still had the eucalyptus branch, so I lifted it up, hoping to use it to hit the ghoulies. When I had it raised above my head, I noticed something strange. The blue glow covering my skin had grown brighter and was crawling up the stick, bright sparks shooting out like magic from a wand.

A loud snarl snapped my attention away from the stick. Some of the ghoulies had noticed me and now had their black-pit eyes pointed in my direction. Swallowing back my fear, I swung the stick, hitting the first one upside the head. It screamed in pain as that strange blue stuff jumped from the stick and onto the ghoulie, sizzling over its skin and making it collapse to the ground into a fit of spasms before turning it to ash. Shocked, I blinked at the stick for a few moments, watching the blue sparks dance some more. Whatever this stuff was, it killed the ghoulies.

Setting my jaw, I went after the others, now backing the poor dog into a corner. I swung my stick like a sword, smacking one after the other, sending them to the ground, screaming and twitching in agony before disintegrating. Eventually, I got to all of them, and Bruno was free. He looked terrified and had a few bite marks on him, but other than that, he seemed okay. I dropped the arm holding the stick, my breath coming in sharp gasps. The dog looked at me with his good eye, his ears still flat in fear, but his tail wagging slowly.

"Good dog," I managed in a shaky voice, holding up my other hand. The blue glow was gone, and my hand shook a little. Suddenly, I was very tired.

Bruno licked my fingers, and I smiled.

"Aiden! Aiden, get over here before that dog bites you!"

I shook my head, Dad's voice cutting through the ringing in my ears. Funny, I hadn't noticed the buzzing sound until now. I turned and looked at my dad. He was standing on the edge of the yard, his hood thrown back, and his face looking serious. He still held onto my twin brothers by their tails, and Logan and Bradley were standing next to him, gawking at me as if I had grown my own tail. And then I stiffened. Had they seen what happened? Did they see the strange blue glow on my skin?

With no other options, I shuffled over to them.

"Let's get home," was all Dad said, turning us all in the right direction.

"Dude, Aiden," Logan murmured as we headed up the street. "What were you doing?"

"I can't believe you did that. You know Mom and Dad always tell us not to tease dogs, especially ones that are barking at us!" Bradley put in, taking a hold of my stick and tossing it aside.

"Were you trying to get him to play fetch or something?" Logan asked.

So, they hadn't seen after all. I shrugged, feeling that was the safest answer for the time being.

Ten minutes later, we were all piling into the living room. Mom greeted us all in her witch costume, asking us if we saw any ghosts or goblins on our nightly adventure. Bradley and Logan got busy telling her everything, which gave me time to gather my thoughts. Despite how terrified I was at seeing the strange red mist and then the armies of ghoulies, I was very proud of myself for helping Bruno.

"Okay, okay, you can tell me the rest in the morning. You guys stayed out later than usual, and it's time for bed."

My brothers groaned again but didn't argue with Mom. Personally, I was more than happy to comply. Fifteen minutes later, my teeth were brushed, my pajamas were on and I was tucked safe and sound in my bed. As I lay there, waiting for sleep to come to me, I thought about that strange blue glow to my skin that had traveled along the stick I'd used to hit the ghoulies. Below the sheets, I lifted my hand

and splayed the fingers in front of my face. The blue glow had returned, and small tendrils of brighter turquoise crackled along my fingertips. I didn't know what this strange stuff was, but I knew that from now on, I wouldn't be so afraid of the ghoulies anymore. With a self-satisfied smile, I let out a long sigh and closed my eyes, content in knowing my dreams would not be haunted again for a long while.

Acknowledgments

Once again, I'd like to thank my family and friends who understand what it takes to be an author, and for not holding it against me. Also, thank you to Monica Castagnasso, my fabulous editor, for taking the time to squeeze this project into her busy schedule. And finally many thanks to my readers, for encouraging me to get this small glimpse into Aiden's life, as brief as it may be, into the hands of those always looking for more tales from the Otherworld.

About The Author

Jenna Elizabeth Johnson grew up and still resides on the Central Coast of California, the very location that has become the set of her novel, Faelorehn, and the inspiration for her other series, The Legend of Oescienne.

Miss Johnson has a degree in Art Practice with an emphasis in Celtic Studies from the University of California at Berkeley. She now draws much of her insight from the myths and legends of ancient Ireland to help set the theme for her books.

Besides writing and drawing, Miss Johnson enjoys reading, gardening, camping and hiking. In her free time (the time not dedicated to writing), she also practices the art of long sword combat and traditional archery.

For contact information, visit the author's website at:
www.jennaelizabethjohnson.com

Connect with me Online

Twitter: @AuthorJEJohnson
Facebook: https://www.facebook.com/authorjejohnson
My Website: http://www.jennaelizabethjohnson.com/
Pinterest: http://www.pinterest.com/authorjejohnson/
Instagram: http://instagram.com/authorjejohnson
Goodreads: https://www.goodreads.com/authorjejohnson
Wattpad: https://www.wattpad.com/user/AuthorJEJohnson

Other Books by This Author

Made in the USA
Lexington, KY
30 July 2019